ORCA
YOUNG
READERS

S0-ABB-081

Seconds

Sylvia Taekema

ORCA BOOK PUBLISHERS

Library and Archives Canada Cataloguing in Publication

Taekema, Sylvia, 1964-
Seconds / Sylvia Taekema.
(Orca young readers)

Issued also in electronic formats.
ISBN 978-1-4598-0403-6

I. Title. II. Series: Orca young readers
PS8639.A25S43 2013   jC813'.6   C2013-901904-9

First published in the United States, 2013
Library of Congress Control Number: 2013935377

Summary: Jake is a dedicated young runner who is fed up with always getting second place.

  MIX
Paper from
responsible sources
FSC® C004071
www.fsc.org

 ANCIENT FOREST ™
FRIENDLY

*Orca Book Publishers is dedicated to preserving the environment and has printed this book on
Forest Stewardship Council® certified paper.*

Orca Book Publishers gratefully acknowledges the support for its publishing programs
provided by the following agencies: the Government of Canada through the
Canada Book Fund and the Canada Council for the Arts, and the Province of
British Columbia through the BC Arts Council and the Book Publishing Tax Credit.

Cover artwork by René Milot
Author photo by Denise Blommestyn

ORCA BOOK PUBLISHERS
PO Box 5626, Stn. B
Victoria, BC Canada
V8R 6S4

ORCA BOOK PUBLISHERS
PO Box 468
Custer, WA USA
98240-0468

www.orcabook.com
Printed and bound in Canada.

16 15 14 13 • 4 3 2 1

For Mark

Chapter One

Jake hated every minute of it. The tension of those few seconds before the gun went off. The elbows that jabbed into his ribs as he jockeyed for a good position. The way the long grass pulled at him, branches grabbed at him, mud sucked at his shoes and sprayed up around him. The way his chest hurt and his head pounded. The way the muscles in his legs screamed at him to quit. The agony of the hills, the monotony of the long straight stretches, the pain of stubbing his toes or rolling an ankle on stones or stumps. The icy water of the swollen creek that was too wide to jump over cleanly, which seeped into his socks and pooled in the bottom of his shoes, making them squish with every step. He hated running, but he wasn't going to quit.

He was going to beat Spencer Solomon today no matter what. Spencer had won the first city race last time out, but only because Jake hadn't been ready. He had been new to the course and the league and hadn't known what to expect. Not this time.

His breathing grew more ragged as he pushed harder, and spit clung to his chin. He was closing the gap, but Spencer still had five meters on him. Three. Now two. And only three hundred meters to the finish. *Time. To. Go.* Jake willed himself to maintain the brutal pace for just a little longer. He knew he could catch Spencer as they tackled the last hill. Stay with him, he thought. Just stay—but Spencer took off in a sprint. How did he do that? Jake gritted his teeth through the mud kicked up by Spencer's spikes. *Run. Run.* He battled up the hill and pushed across the line. Sucking in great gulps of air, he ripped his racing number away from the pins, crumpled it into a ball and threw it on the ground. He lifted his shirt and wiped the mud from his face. Second. Again.

Jake walked around for a bit, until his breathing had slowed and he'd calmed down. Next time. He'd get past Spencer next time. He went over the course in his head. He could probably shave a few seconds off his time on the flat stretches, but what he really needed to do was find a way to get up the hills more quickly. He made his way back toward the bike racks to grab the water bottle and the sweatshirt he'd left in a back-pack slung over his bike handle. He almost tripped over some kid sitting on the curb changing his shoes.

"Hey, Jake."

Jake regained his balance, straightened up and turned. "Simon?"

Simon Patterson. They used to be neighbors. He and Simon had done all kinds of stuff together, from Lego to video games. Simon had had a great tree house. They'd spent hours there—even tried spending the night in it once but were scared out by an owl. They had built massive Tinkertoy robots in Simon's basement and had some great movie nights at Jake's. They'd throw new pizza ideas at Jake's dad, and he'd cook up a masterpiece every time. Some were great, like the triple-cheese-goo experiment. Some were weird, like the one with the marshmallows.

Then Jake had moved across town, about two and a half years ago now. His dad had wanted a house with a workshop. Simon came over to the new place a couple of times. This was at the height of Jake's hockey craze.

Jake watched all the games, knew all the teams and most of the players, and bought all the cards. He wanted to play, but the equipment was expensive and the practice schedule was too hard to fit in. Running was easier that way. Simon hadn't loved hockey the way Jake had. Although Jake still liked to watch the games on TV with his dad, he wasn't a hockey nut anymore. He probably hadn't seen Simon in over a year. He remembered him as kind of tubby and klutzy. Always ready with a funny line. Wore glasses and Spiderman shirts. He'd loved Spiderman.

"Simon! Long time no see! What are you doing here?"

Simon looked up. Same curly blond hair. Glasses. Red T-shirt. "Running."

"Yeah? I didn't take you for a runner. No offense."

Simon laughed. "That's okay. I didn't either. I started because my mom made me. *It's not a complicated sport*, she said. I think she meant you don't have to be coordinated to do this sport." He laughed again. "But now, I like it."

"Yeah? What place did you get?"

"Thirty-sixth."

Thirty-sixth? Yikes. What was there to like about being thirty-sixth? thought Jake.

"Last week I was fortieth. So thirty-sixth is okay. I felt good today."

Well, there's your problem, thought Jake. If you're running hard, hard enough to be up front and not back at thirty-sixth, you don't feel good. You feel like garbage. Like I do now.

"How did you do?" asked Simon.

Jake scowled. "Second."

"Second? That's amazing. You always were good at running."

Not good enough, thought Jake, feeling the anger return. "Yeah, well, it's only because the guy in first cut me off."

"That stinks," said Simon.

"Look at me," said Jake. "Thanks to Spencer Solomon, I'm covered in mud."

"The course sure is muddy today. Pigs could wallow in some parts. Spencer won? Are you sure he cut you off?"

"Yep."

"I've never seen him do anything like that."

How would you know? thought Jake. You probably couldn't see much of anything from back where you were. "That's how it looked to me," he said.

Chapter Two

The next Tuesday afternoon, another hundred or so runners, including Jake and Spencer, were back on the course. It was the third race of six scheduled runs before the championship, and Spencer was well in front. The previous year, when Jake had run for his school team, he had won every race easily. His coach had told him he should run in the city-league races. Said he had a good chance of winning. *Right*.

Jake was angry. His chest was burning. His legs felt like lead. What was he doing wrong? He was eating right, drinking lots. He was running every morning at six, almost twice the distance of the course, and it wasn't helping him at all. He watched Spencer's bright-green shoes disappear over a ridge.

Dig deep, Jake told himself. Dig deep. But it wasn't enough. The bridge, the hill, the finish. He crossed the line in second place. He saw Spencer off to the left, walking in slow circles with his hands on his hips. A strange feeling began to bubble up inside Jake's chest.

"Good run," said the official at the line.

Jake nodded. Then he blurted out, "That guy with the green shoes? He pushed me. Almost knocked me right off the course. Cost me a lot of time."

Jake was almost as surprised by his words as the official was. "The first-place guy? Pushing?"

"Ah, yeah."

"That's a serious charge, son." He looked Jake straight in the eye. Jake met his gaze for a few seconds, then put his head down, hands on his knees, and tried to slow his breathing. He was winded.

"I'll look into it. Whereabouts on the course?"

"Ah, not sure," Jake said. "About three quarters of the way maybe?" He looked up again. "Never mind. The race is done. It doesn't matter anymore."

"No, no. We take these things seriously. Stick around. I'll get back to you."

Jake still felt strange as he went to get his gear. He might have pushed it a little far today.

"Hey, Jake." Simon was sitting on the curb again, changing his shoes.

"Simon."

"How'd you do today?"

Jake held up two fingers. "You?"

"Thirty-three, that's me." Simon beamed.

Jake sat down beside Simon. He nodded absently. "I'm pretty sure I could come in first if I had fancy spikes like Spencer's. I wanted shoes like that, but my dad wouldn't buy them for me. He says they're too expensive and I'll just outgrow them."

"That's probably true," said Simon. "Your spikes don't look too bad, just experienced."

"Maybe, but it's not fair. Those new shoes give Spencer a big advantage."

"They sure look cool," Simon agreed. He waited. "Maybe Spencer's just fast, Jake."

"And I'm not?"

"I didn't say that. Second place is no disgrace. I don't mind that he got new shoes." Simon smiled. "He gave me his old ones. I used to just wear my running shoes, but spikes make a big difference." Simon held up the underside of one shoe and laughed. "If you get my *point*."

Jake didn't. "You asked him for his shoes?"

"No. He offered them to me. They didn't fit him anymore, and they fit me pretty good so..."

"So you took them?" Jake couldn't believe what he was hearing.

"Well, he wasn't going to use them anymore. I thought it was a nice thing to do."

Jake shook his head. "Simon, can't you see what he's doing?"

"Being a nice guy?"

"No, man! He's putting you down, Simon. He's showing you you're not as good as him."

"I'm *not* as good as him!"

"Well, I am," muttered Jake. "And next week, he'll know it."

The official Jake had spoken to after the race came over. Jake sighed. He wished he hadn't said anything. He looked up.

"I talked to the other runner, son. Says he didn't do any pushing."

"I figured he'd say that," said Jake.

"Right. So I talked to my course monitors," said the official. "They say they didn't see anybody doing any pushing." He paused briefly before going on.

"In fact, they say they never saw you and the other fellow close enough to each other for any pushing to be going on." He waited.

Jake didn't know what to say. He didn't know what had come over him to make him say he'd been pushed, except that for a moment it had seemed a good way to push Spencer out of first place. "I—I guess it's hard to see everything," replied Jake sheepishly.

The official frowned, then nodded. "You can be sure we'll keep watching things closely." He walked away. Jake walked the other way, toward his bike. He could feel Simon looking at him, but he didn't look back.

As he knelt to unlock his bike, Jake heard footsteps on the gravel and glanced up.

"Dad?"

"Hey, Jake. Good race?"

"It was okay, I guess. Uh, I thought I told you and Mom you didn't have to come to the runs."

"You did." His dad smiled. His eyes were twinkling.

"Not a lot of people usually come out. Runners need to focus on the race, without any distractions."

His dad watched the steady stream of cars pulling out onto the road. "Looks like a lot of people came out today." He smiled again. "You want a ride?"

"I have my bike."

"Right. I'll see you at home then."

Jake finished unlocking his bike. It was true. He'd read more than once how a serious runner could not let anything break his concentration. Still, he felt a little sad as he heard his dad walk away.

Chapter Three

"Jake!"

Jake heard his mother calling him, but he was in the middle of a workout in the basement and didn't feel like stopping. He couldn't be in trouble. He'd taken out the garbage and fed the cats. Maybe she didn't really need him and if he just waited, she would forget she'd called. Or maybe she'd call his older brother, Luke, instead. He just listened to music all day and fooled around on his guitar. Hopefully his mom would remember Luke was home too.

"Jake!" she hollered again. Guess not.

Jake grabbed a towel and made his way up the stairs.

His mother was standing in the middle of the kitchen, surrounded by grocery bags. The freezer door hung open, and she was holding the fridge door open with her toe. She balanced in front of it with a head of lettuce in one hand and a bag of frozen peas in the other.

"Yes?"

She turned to look at him. "Jake, what is all this?"

"Oh. Yeah. My water bottles. I need to be ready for training and races. And I made ice cubes out of my sports drinks so I can just drop them into the cold water. Sports drinks are good, but they're better diluted, so I thought up the ice-cube idea."

"Uh-huh. Clever. And this?" She tilted her head toward the wall of green jars in the fridge.

"Ah." Jake's eyes lit up. "The secret ingredient to running success. Pickles."

"Pickles are the key to running success?"

"Yes. I've read all about it, Mom. Pickle power. Pre-race days, you eat pickles. On race day itself, you just do the juice."

"You drink it?"

"Yep."

"Pickle juice?"

"Yep."

"That's disgusting."

"I know, but they say that pickle juice is very effective in preventing cramps."

"Uh-huh. Who knew? But where am I supposed to put my groceries?"

Jake shrugged. "You could buy another fridge," he suggested with half a smile.

His mother laughed. "How about you store one jar of pickles, one or two bottles of water and one tray of supercubes at a time, instead of a three-year supply? And keep the rest in the basement?"

Jake rolled his eyes. "I guess." He sighed. "But then I'll constantly have to monitor the inventory."

Now his mother rolled her eyes. "You sound like one of those magazine articles you're always reading." She put on a serious face and deepened her voice. "I'll help you keep tabs on it and let you know when you need to replenish your stock." Then she smiled and tossed him the lettuce. "Deal?"

Jake caught it and grinned. "Okay. Deal. Did you buy granola bars?"

"Again? I thought I bought a jumbo box last week."

"They're gone. And so are the bananas. I need to have lots of bananas."

"I see. Jake, it's not the Olympics, you know. Are you sure you're not taking this running stuff a bit too seriously?"

"No. If you're going to do something, you might as well do it right. Isn't that what you and Dad always say? This is important stuff, Mom. It's a science. Would you like it better if I was eating junk food?"

"No." She smiled and messed up his hair. "No, I would not. I'll get you those bananas, as long as you remember that a little monkey business now and then is okay."

"Can I go back downstairs now? I was in the middle of a workout."

"Sure, but help me unpack these bags first."

"Aww, Mom."

"Consider it part of your workout, mister."

Jake tucked a jar of peanut butter under his arm and grabbed two loaves of bread. "Hey, Mom," he said as he made his way over to the cupboard to put them away. "Guess who's running in the city league?"

"Who?" she asked, kneeling in front of the fridge taking pickle jars out.

"Simon Patterson."

"Simon? Really? How's he doing? You boys haven't seen each other for ages. Why don't you invite him over sometime?"

"I don't know, Mom. Simon seems like a bit of a..." Jake paused. The word *loser* was on the tip of his tongue.

His mother turned. "A what?"

"Nothing. It's just been a long time, that's all."

Chapter Four

This was it. Jake felt it. Today he was going to win. Everyone was gathered at the starting line. There were a lot of runners out today, but he was only interested in one. And there he was, about three meters down the line. Chatting it up with the guys beside him. Mr. Green Spikes himself. "You're going down today," whispered Jake. "Somebody's going down, and it isn't going to be me." It made Jake feel kind of bad when he said this, but it made him feel tough too, and he knew he'd have to be tough out there.

The official called all runners to the line. Jake got ready. A good start was key.

"Ready," shouted the official. He raised his gun. *Steady.* A group of about ten runners popped the line just ahead of the gun. Barely, but still. False start, thought Jake, and he relaxed again at the line. He waited for the runners to return, but they kept going. They weren't coming back! He looked at the official.

"False start!" he yelled.

The official shook his head and waved him on. "Go!" he hollered.

"You've got to be kidding!" Jake grumbled as he kicked into high gear.

This was bad. Usually he started out in the top ten, but now he'd have to plow his way through everybody. He caught up to the crowd at the end of the field. Then the path narrowed, and it was steep on both sides. There was nowhere to pass. A heavyset runner in front of him blocked Jake's way and his view. He was breathing heavily and swayed from side to side when he ran. Move, thought Jake, move! Finally things opened up, and Jake edged by the swayer and at least a dozen other runners. But there were still so many in front of him. Just ahead he saw the familiar flash of the green shoes. Spencer. Good. He wasn't far ahead.

Bit by bit, Jake started to move up. The mob ducked back into the forest on the part of the trail that snaked uphill. Trees lined the path on both sides.

Runners ahead started to slow. Now what? Keep going! There was activity off to one side. Someone was down. It happened easily in a crunch like this. He'd have to be careful not to trip. Wait. Simon? Was it Simon? It *was* Simon. Jake recognized the red T-shirt. What had happened? There was blood on his face. His glasses were missing. Runners were chugging by slowly, like cars passing an accident scene. He should stop. Simon needed help. But there was no time for that now. It probably looked worse than it was, and Jake was no paramedic anyway. Plus, there were monitors who would help. It was their job.

There was a narrow path just off the main trail. Jake saw his chance and slid past the crowd. Maybe Spencer was still caught in the crush of runners. He hoped so. He had to keep moving. He passed another runner. Then a group of four and then another two. Now he was all alone. He ran downhill out of the big trees and over a set of smaller hills in the scrub. He followed the trail through the high grass along the creek. *Focus. Focus. Look ahead. Breathe. Breathe.* He kept thinking he'd come up behind another runner, but there was no one. It's mine, thought Jake. It's mine. Yes! He'd played it smart, and it had paid off.

All the sweeter because of the slow start. *Keep up the pace. Keep up the pace.* He could see the flags of the finish line off in the distance. Maybe five hundred meters. Over the bridge and then up the hill on the other side. *Come on.* His legs were heavy. His throat ached.

Jake heard him before he saw him. Heard his feet land on the gravel just before the bridge. Heard him breathing, deeply but evenly. Someone was coming up behind him, fast. *Come on. Come on.* He wanted to look back, but he couldn't afford the time it would cost him. He crossed the bridge and ducked under some low trees. *Come on.* One hundred meters to the finish. Only one hundred meters. *Stay ahead. Stay ahead.* He climbed the final hill in short strides. *Push, push. Don't slow down.* I am not eating mud today, he vowed. I am not. Fifty meters. Twenty. Ten. Almost. Almost. At seven meters he saw the green shoes. At three meters he felt mud spray up beside him. He threw himself across the line, but Spencer had beaten him by a step. A second. Second.

Chapter Five

Jake plunked himself down on the curb beside Simon. "What happened?" he asked.

Simon had a wicked scratch across his cheek and a purple goose egg on his forehead.

"Caught a branch in the face. Stupid. I should have known. There are always low branches there."

"Hurt?"

"Some. My pride, mostly. My glasses got knocked off in the close encounter with the tree, and when I went off the trail to get them I slipped in the mud and smacked my head on a rock. Little bit of rock and roll."

Jake smiled. "Rock and roll, huh? You should come jam with Luke sometime."

Simon laughed. "How'd you do?"

Jake scowled. "Second," he muttered. "Aargh," he groaned, flopping back on the grass.

"You must have had a great run then," said Simon.

"What do you mean?"

"I didn't see you ahead of me when we took off, so I turned around to see if I could find you in the crowd. When I looked behind me, everyone was coming at me like a freight train. Better keep moving, I thought. When I turned around again, boom! I hit the branch head on. Stopped me right in my tracks."

"You were looking for me?" Jake sat up again. He studied the angry mark on Simon's cheek. "Look, I would have stopped, but I had to take my chance to get through that crowd. It was a false start, you know. That's what set me back in the first place."

"False start? What is this, the Olympics?"

Jake shook his head and laughed. "You sound like my mom."

Simon gave him a lopsided grin. "Anyway, that's okay. Max Chen helped me out. He found my glasses for me and then found a course monitor."

Max? He was usually in the top ten.

"Sure you're okay?"

"Yep."

"See you next week?"

"Yep."

On the way to his bike, Jake glanced at the results board taped on the wall of the picnic shelter. He looked for Max Chen's name: #33. Ouch. Max could have let someone else look after Simon. The monitors would have gotten there without him. All they had to do was help Simon off the course. Then Jake saw something that surprised him. At #96, Simon Patterson. Simon had finished the race, goose egg and all, and #96 was not the last runner in.

Chapter Six

"Jake, dinner!"

"Coming." Jake left the running magazine on his desk and headed downstairs. There was an article in it on mental toughness that he wanted to finish. Toughness. That was what he needed to focus on. His back ached a little and the muscles in his legs felt tight going down the steps. He'd added a second run to his daily routine, and his body wasn't used to that yet. A lot of the articles talked about gradual training, alternating easier workouts and rest days, but Jake couldn't see how that made any sense. Rest days? How was he going to win if he took it easy? No, he was going to be the toughest one out there. That's how he would win.

He entered the kitchen. "Come on, Jake." His mom smiled. "Dad made his world-famous tacos. We want to eat them while they're hot."

"Oh, no worries there, gang," called his dad, wearing the Taco-won-do Master apron he'd gotten for his last birthday. It had a picture of a cartoon guy with a black belt juggling tomatoes while snap-kicking a head of lettuce. "They're HOT, all right."

"Tacos?" Jake looked over at his mother, who was pouring glasses of water. "Mom, I told you last week I can't eat spicy food. I need pasta. Lots of pasta. And rice."

"Jake." His mom laughed. "We've had spaghetti three times in the last week. It'll be good to have something different. And Dad's tacos are the best! Come on. Sit down."

Jake sat. But he didn't fill up his taco shell. His brother, Luke, was waving a bowl of shredded cheese in front of his face, but Jake didn't take it. "Serious runners don't eat spicy food."

"Uh-huh. So what's stopping *you* from eating it?" Luke grinned. Jake glared at him. "Okay, okay, more for me." Luke shrugged, setting the bowl down in front of himself. "I like tacos."

Me too, thought Jake. But…he sighed. "Is it okay if I just have peanut-butter-and-banana sandwiches?" He looked at his mom.

She looked at his dad. "Ask Dad. He's the chef today."

"Dad?"

"Sure, sport, but you don't know what you're missing." He winked.

Jake went to the cupboard. "Mom, we need more peanut butter."

"Put it on the list."

"And more bread. The whole-grain stuff."

"Right."

"And chocolate milk. Chocolate milk is key for post-race recovery. So lots of chocolate milk."

"Yes, your highness."

"Oh, and Mom," cut in Luke in a commanding voice, "we need more pretzels. Pretzels are perfect for post-practice recovery."

"And ice cream," Jake's dad added. "Ice cream is ideal for post-taco recovery." He wiped his forehead. "Whew. These are hot, all right! Bring on the butter-scotch ripple."

Jake looked around. They were laughing! He knew he was going to have to work on being mentally tough, but he didn't realize he'd need it to deal with his own family.

"What's so funny?" he asked.

"Oh, we're not laughing at you, Jake-O. We're laughing with you," said Luke, grinning.

"Sure, except I'm not laughing."

"Well, then, maybe we're laughing for you, Jakey. I think you may have forgotten how," said his dad with a smile.

Jake suddenly felt frustrated. They just didn't get it. "Look," he said. "I need food for fuel. Good food. The right food. What's the problem with that?"

"Nothing, Jake. Nothing at all."

"I eat to run. I take running seriously. Running is good for you."

"Yes," said his mother softly. There was a hint of worry in her eyes. "It's supposed to be."

Chapter Seven

Jake was grumpy. He had managed to push himself for another fifteen minutes in his evening run, but it hadn't come easy. He felt like a fish out of water, gasping for air. His mom was sitting at the table, reading the paper, when he came in. "Hey, Jake. Did you see the construction at the corner?"

"No. What corner?"

"They're putting up a new restaurant. On the corner of our street and Swift. It's going to be called Sl-ice."

"Why are you saying Sl-ice?"

"That's the way it's written. See?"

Jake looked at the ad she held in her hand. *Opening soon. Sl'ice. Your Pizza and Ice Cream Perfectorium.*

"S-ounds g-ood, don't you think? I doubt they'll offer as many pizza toppings as Dad does, but as long as they have butterscotch ripple, we should be okay in the ice-cream department."

So that's what Simon had been talking about. He had called just before Jake went out, mentioning a new pizza place, but Jake had cut him off. He'd been in a hurry.

"Wanna go when it opens up?" Simon had asked.

"Umm, I'm pretty busy these days," Jake had answered. "And I'm pretty careful about what I eat too."

"Oh, okay."

Jake would explain to Simon next time he saw him. He sure didn't feel like pizza or ice cream now. He had a headache, and his knees hurt. "Ah, Mom, I'm going to take a shower and then go to bed, okay?" Jake made his way to the stairs but stopped with his foot on the bottom step. He heard music coming from Luke's room. "Ugh. He plays that guitar all the time," grumbled Jake. "Who can get any sleep around here?"

His mother looked at him, eyebrows raised slightly. "What's the matter, Jake?"

"Nothing. I'm just tired, that's all."

Jake plodded upstairs. His mother followed, but when she got to the top, she went the other way down the hallway to Luke's room. Soon it was quiet. Thanks, Mom, Jake thought. He dropped his jacket on his bed. It made a crinkling noise. He pulled a piece of paper out of the pocket. Last week's spelling test. Thirteen out of twenty-five. Oh yeah. Yikes. He'd been so busy, he'd forgotten to review for it. He didn't think Mrs. Bradley could keep him out of city-league running because of his grades, but his mother just might. He knew he'd better be ready for this week's test. He practiced the words as he stood under the warm spray of the shower. *Flight, f-l-i-g-h-t. Journey, j-o-u-r-n-e-y. Accident, a-c-c-i-d-e-n-t. Friendship, f-r-e-i-n-d-s-h-i-p.* Or was it *f-r-i-e-n-d-s-h-i-p*? He was tired. Did it really matter?

Chapter Eight

Okay, if some guys wanted to jump the start today, Jake was going with them. This was it. He was ready. He was focused. He didn't even bother looking to see where Spencer was in the lineup. He moved right at the gun and got out front early. No one would pass him today. No one. This was his race. He had to give it his all. He ignored the ache in his gut. He ignored the fire in his chest. Be tough, he told himself. Be tough. So far he didn't hear any footsteps behind him, but his heart was pounding so hard he wasn't sure he'd hear them anyway. He wiped the sweat from his face and kept putting one foot in front of the other. *Don't let up. Don't let up.* Up the hill. Through the trees. *Watch out for low branches. One foot in front of the other.* Down the hill.

Along the creek. His stomach clenched. His leg muscles strained and stretched. *Never mind! Be tough. One foot in front of the other. Push. Harder. Push. Harder.* His fingers tingled. His feet were numb. It hurt to breathe. He pounded across the flat stretches. He forced himself up the hills. *Don't let up. Don't slow down. Up. Down. Steady. Steady. Focus. Keep running. Look ahead. Keep running. Look ahead. Don't think about anything else but putting one foot in front of the other.* Finally, Jake could see the bridge. His vision started to swim and things began to float around. There were little stars dancing in front of him. *Dig. Dig. Up the hill. One foot in front of the other.* One foot in front of the other until…until he stepped right over the finish line.

First. First! He had won! He knew he could do it. He knew it. He threw his head back, trying to draw in enough air, and walked around a bit. The official at the line was giving him the thumbs-up and saying something to him, but he couldn't make it out so he just nodded. He wanted to wait around at the finish line to see who would come in next. He wanted to see those green shoes come across the line. There was no one yet. No one. This was incredible. Unbelievable.

He had nailed it! He felt great. He felt fantastic. He felt...terrible. Before Jake could see who came in next, he had to get out of there. Fast. He had to find a bathroom, a spot in the woods, somewhere. He was going to be sick.

Whew. Better. Jake sat up against a tree for a while and then, when he felt a little stronger, he wandered down to the picnic shelter to see if the results had been posted. And there it was: *#1 Jake Jarvis*. He stared at it. The letters looked 3-D, and he imagined big beams of light shooting out of them. Jake smiled and took in a few deep, slow breaths. He saw Simon sitting on the curb and strolled over to him. Jake had his hands up behind his head. He felt really lousy. He was shaky and his insides were in knots and his head felt like a big echoey cave, but he tried not to let on.

"Hey, Simon." He sat down, but not too close. His breath smelled like pickles. He definitely felt better sitting.

"Jake."

"Good race today?"

"Excellent. I came in at twenty-five, and I'm still alive. Moving up just a little bit every time."

Jake nodded. He waited. He wanted to tell Simon he had won.

"It was a great day for a run, wasn't it?" Simon continued. "The sun's out for once. The birds are singing."

"The birds?"

"Yeah. Ever notice how many different types of birds there are in this forest?"

"No."

"And all the different kinds of trees?"

"Like the one that reached out and grabbed you last week?" Jake grabbed Simon's arm just above the elbow, then punched him lightly on the shoulder. He was glad to see the mark on Simon's face had faded quite a bit.

Simon laughed. "It was a sugar maple, I think, but I'm going out on a limb there. Get it? Limb? I've been thinking maybe I'll branch out and become a comic. Ha ha. Branch out? What do you think?"

"Uh-huh." Jake waited. He really wanted to tell Simon he had won.

"There are animals too. Last week there was a snake. This week there were rabbits. These are hoppy trails, you know."

Jake was getting impatient. "I'm not here to look at the wildlife, Simon. I'm focused on the finish line."

"Well, there's a lot more going on out there than just the running."

"Maybe, but you don't win that way!"

"I think you do."

Simon squinted at the long line of cars pulling out onto the highway. "Hey, does your dad still drive a green Jetta? Was he here? I haven't seen him in a long time."

Jake looked at the cars, then shook his head. "Nah, he doesn't usually come out." He paused for a moment. "Anyway, I had my eyes on the prize and it's mine today." He stood up, hands on his hips in a kind of superhero pose. His stomach cramped. He tried to make his grimace pass for a grin.

"Oh yeah? First? Way to go!" Simon stuck up his hand for a high five.

Jake slapped it. "Yep, I knew I could beat that Spencer Solomon."

"Ahh."

"It was just a matter of time. Just a matter of wearing him down. He's all show, no go, you know," said Jake. He thought Simon might appreciate the wordplay.

"Uh, actually," said Simon, "Spencer's not here today."

"What?"

"He's sick."

"Sick?" Jake was reminded of his own queasy stomach. He sat down again. "Not likely! Scared, maybe!"

"Nope. Not chicken, just the chicken pox."

"Get out! Chicken pox is for little kids!"

"He never got it when he was little. Guess he picked it up from his younger sister."

"No way." Jake remembered having chicken pox in kindergarten. He and Simon had had it at the same time. The first couple days were not so fun, but after that they'd spent most of a week watching cartoons and building Hot Wheels tracks together. They'd tied together a bunch of elastics and made a great bungee jump for their Lego people. "Geronimo!" they'd hollered before every jump. It had been fun.

"Wait a minute," said Jake. He was beginning to feel angry. This was not turning out the way it was supposed to. "How come you know so much about Spencer anyway?"

"He's my neighbor."

"He doesn't live in that neighborhood. I should know. That used to be *my* neighborhood."

"He moved into your old house!"

"What? A family named Johannsen moved into my house."

"Yeah, the Johannsens moved in, and then they moved out a year later when their dad got transferred. That's when Spence moved in."

"Spence, huh. You guys tight?"

"Not really."

"You guys over at each other's places all the time?"

Simon eyed Jake a minute. "Now and then he hollers, *Hey, Patty, want to shoot some hoops in the driveway?*"

"Patty? What, like hamburger patty, potato patty? You let him call you names?"

"No, Patty like Patterson, which is my last name, if you remember. It's what you used to call me when you hollered over the fence."

They were both quiet for a second. This was not turning out at all the way it was supposed to, thought Jake. "What have you got against the guy anyway?" asked Simon with a sigh.

Well, the fact that he beats me all the time and when I finally beat him I find out he wasn't actually in the race, thought Jake, but he didn't say it.

"I'm going home," Jake said finally.

"Me too." Simon stood up and slung his backpack over one shoulder. It was faded and scuffed. Spiderman looked out at Jake as Simon turned.

Jake shook his head. "Aren't you a little old for that Spiderman backpack?"

"Never. It's a classic! Love what you love, man."

"I love running," Jake said.

"No, you don't." Simon laughed. "You love winning."

Jake shrugged. "Is there a problem with winning?" he asked. "Isn't that the whole idea?"

Simon smiled, a little sadly. "Good run today, Jake. See you later."

"Yeah." As Jake passed the results board, he saw his name again at number one, but the 3-D effect and the beams of light seemed to have vanished.

Chapter Nine

When he got home, Jake told his mother he was tired and asked if he could skip dinner until later. She felt his forehead and ruffled his hair and asked if he was okay. He nodded and went to his room. He looked up chicken pox on his computer. Simon was right— it didn't just affect little kids. In fact, it was usually worse for kids who got it when they were older. Leave it to Spencer to ruin the race by not coming. He ruined everything. He had Jake's shoes. He lived in Jake's house. He probably had Jake's room! He'd stolen Jake's friend! Jake knew this wasn't true, but he didn't care. He had come in first, and it didn't even count. If Spencer had been there, Jake might still have won. Or he might not have. He'd given every ounce of energy to that run. He didn't think he could run like that again. And now, even if Spencer did come back and Jake beat him, he wouldn't know if it was for real or if being sick had set Spencer back. Who got chicken pox when they were twelve? In the middle of cross-country season? It bothered Jake that he had won and it wasn't good enough. It bothered him that he might not *be* good enough. It bothered him that people didn't seem to take things seriously. Chicken pox. Puns. Jokes. Snakes. Rabbits. Spiderman.

He looked around the room. It bothered him that he had striped curtains and Spencer Solomon probably had the hockey ones hanging in his old room. It bothered him that he was unbelievably hungry, but his stomach still hurt so much he didn't think he could eat anything. It bothered him that there might not be anything downstairs that he actually wanted to eat. He didn't even want to think about spaghetti or anything with peanut butter. It bothered him that all of this bothered him. What was the matter with him? Something had to change.

He had some spelling words he needed to look over. He had some magazine articles he wanted to read. He had to figure out how to intensify his training program even more. But he didn't want to. He didn't want to do anything. He was tired. So he just sat on his bed for a long time. After a while, his mother called up the stairs that the phone was for him. He glanced over at the clock on his bedside table. The glowing numbers told him it was already seven thirty. He'd been sitting in the dark. He hadn't even noticed.

dark-haired, short and stocky. He looked
[c]ould simply power his way to the finish.
[the]e all wearing matching jerseys, silver with
[a diamond]-shaped logo on the front made out of four
[triangles,] two black, two royal blue. The two small
[trian]gles were stylized running shoes. The two
[oth]er triangles resembled racing flags. The
[dia]mond ran in block letters along one edge.
[Da]ve had given Jake a jersey, but he wished
[he'd p]rovided shoes too. He looked down at his
[sho]es and then at those of the other guys. Six of
[them] looked as scuffed as his. But one pair was
[bright] green. One of the runners was wearing the
[sam]e green spikes Spencer had. Jake looked up.
[He k]new it. Sam was the one he'd have to watch.
["Okay,] fellas," said Dave, "now that you all know
[me], what do you say we get started?"

The [C]edar Grove Conservation area had a long
[trail] of woods and grassy meadows that rolled
[down to] the river. After doing a series of warm-up
[runs, t]he boys started running along the path down
[to the wa]ter and then followed it up into the woods,
[over rid]ges and along the edge of a pumpkin field.
[Most of t]he field had been cleared already, but one

Chapter Ten

"Hello?"

"Jake?"

"Yes."

"Hi. It's Dave Driscoll here. I'm with the Diamond Running Club."

Jake had heard of them. What did Dave Driscoll want to talk to him about? "Okay."

"We've been invited to an event in Deep Rapids next Saturday, and we can take a team of five runners. I've got four. Heard you were the top-place runner in your division in the city league. We're wondering if you'd like to join us."

"Are you sure you're not looking for Spencer Solomon?"

"Who?"

"The top-place runner."

"Is this Jake Jarvis?"

"Yes."

"I've got a list here with your name on top. Look, son, if you're not interested I can call the next guy."

"No, hang on. I'm interested."

"Okay. Let me give you some details. We have a practice tomorrow afternoon. Can you make it?"

"Sure."

Cedar Grove Conservation Area, 4:30.

As Jake was writing the time down on a piece of paper, his dad and Luke came in. Luke danced around the kitchen, playing the counter, the table, the Tupperware and finally the pickle jar inside the fridge like a set of drums. He took out a can of pop, shut the fridge door with his elbow and whirled around, grinning. Jake's dad was leaning against the doorframe, laughing.

"Where did you guys go?" asked Jake.

"A concert. The Cave Dwellers. It was awesome."

"Oh."

Chapter

Shawn Marshall, Paul Biggs
Jake nodded as Dave Drisco
member of the Diamond te
who his stiffest competition
and thin with thick, wavy,
his shoulders. He'd look lik
pale. Jake wondered if Sha
faster if he cut his hair. He w
run faster himself if he cut h
head. Hmmm. He'd have to

Paul was small, even
wise, and full of energy. He
bouncing on his toes, jumpi
Sam was quiet, with a certa

Tony wa
like he
They we
a diamor
triangles
outer tri
larger in
name Di
Sharp. I
the club
worn spi
the shoe
new. An
exact sa
Sam. He
"We
each oth
The
thin stri
out alor
stretche
by the
over br
Most o

section was still full of big bright-orange pumpkins. This is easy, thought Jake. No problem. He stayed easily ahead of Tony and Paul. He moved ahead of Shawn and positioned himself right behind Sam. He thought of passing him but figured he'd just stay behind this time and study his technique. When they came out of the woods again and into the open, Dave waved them over. They weren't stopping already, were they? That was nothing!

When everybody was together again, Dave had them sit in a circle on the grass. This is like kindergarten, thought Jake. Dave started talking to them about how there was more to running a race than just covering the distance. Continuous running helped build endurance, but a runner also needed depth. He needed a well of energy he could tap into at key moments, such as when he needed to pass or to finish strong. To win, thought Jake. Yes. He liked what he was hearing. Dave had the boys spread themselves out in a line across the field and start running as they had been, but when he blew his whistle, they were to do wind sprints, running as hard as they could, as if they were doing the one-hundred-meter dash. When they heard the whistle again, they were to resume their regular pace.

When they had crossed the meadow this way and were back in the woods, they ran a loop that took them back out into the open and they did the sprints again. Jake lost track of how many times they did it. Finally, Dave put the whistle down and told them to finish with an easy run down the path and back to the parking lot where they had started. It was hard work, and Jake ached all over, but his mind told him this was good. Finally, he thought, watching Dave clap each boy on the shoulder as he said goodbye, here was a guy who didn't fool around, who took things seriously.

"Great work out there today, Jake."

"Thanks. See you tomorrow?"

"No. We meet every Monday, Wednesday, Friday, if we can. Take a break tomorrow. We'll see you Friday."

What? Take a break? No way. That wasn't going to take Jake where he wanted to go. Toughness. That was his focus. Still, he was hopeful about the way things had gone that day.

Thursday morning, Jake ran as usual. The muscles in his ankles felt tight after the sprints the day before, but he just ran through the pain. The weather had turned colder, and he puffed out small clouds as he jogged along. After school he was ready to go out again, but his mom stopped him at the door. "It's sleeting, Jake."

"Yeah, I can hear it on the windows."

"I don't want you to go out."

"Why not?"

"It's sleeting, Jake."

"Mom, I can't let a little bit of ice stop me. I have to be ready for anything. What if it's sleeting on race day? I have to be tough."

She crossed her arms and smiled. "It's not race day, buster, and I can be tough too, you know. I don't want you to catch pneumonia. You're not going out."

Jake sighed. "Mothers think everything causes pneumonia." His mother laughed and ruffled his hair. He knew right then that he was going to give up the idea of shaving his head. He liked it when she did that. Jake went downstairs to work out instead. To his surprise, Luke was there, and so was all his stuff. Guitars, amplifiers, cords and wires running everywhere.

"What are you doing here?"

"Mom said it was too noisy for you if I played in my room."

"How am I supposed to work out down here?"

"Do it to the tunes, man!" Luke grinned.

Jake picked up his hand weights. "You know, if Dad's such a fan, you should get him to build you a room over the garage."

"Nice idea, but I don't think it's going to happen."

"C'mon. He loves your music."

"Me, yes." Luke put a hand over his heart. Then he patted his guitar. "This baby, not so much. You know what Dad listens to on the radio in his workshop. Golden oldies and moldies, country tunes and hockey games."

They laughed.

"But he goes to concerts with you. Why would he do that if he didn't want to?"

"Because I don't tell him he can't. Besides, you know that supply of earplugs he keeps on the shelf for when he's using the table saw? He keeps a stash in his jacket pocket too, for when we go out to the bands."

Luke plugged in his guitar. "Why do you have to practice all the time anyway?" Jake asked.

"I'm not practicing, dude. I'm playing."

Chapter Twelve

Friday, the team met at Cedar Grove again. Jake was ready to go and jogged off toward the trees where they'd done the warm-ups the last time, but the guys remained standing in a circle in the parking lot. Dave was leaning against the fence, talking to them. Jake ran back to join them. He didn't want to miss any of the strategy talk, although he was developing his own strategy about how to take on Sam. Stick to him like a shadow the whole way and then slide past him at the finish.

Jake joined the group. They weren't talking strategy. They weren't even talking about running. Tony was talking about his twin sisters and the birthday party they were going to have that weekend.

They were turning four. "Way too much giggling and screaming," complained Tony. "My mom wants me to help, but I don't know if I'll survive." Everyone laughed.

Paul had a music recital that evening. He played the trombone. Shawn talked about a new video game he wanted to try.

"What about you, Sam? What's going on with you?" asked Dave. Sam shrugged slightly and smiled. Paul jumped in and told them how Sam had competed in the Math Olympics at school.

"And?" asked Dave.

Sam grinned and unzipped his jacket to show off a gold medal. Jake knew it. Sam liked to win.

"Sam does fractions for fun," Shawn joked as they all gave Sam a high five. "How about you, Jake?"

"Huh? Oh, I…" He paused. "I run."

"No gaming?" asked Shawn.

"Not much."

"No long division?" Sam added. Everyone laughed.

"No little sisters?" asked Tony.

"No music lessons?" asked Paul at the same time.

"No, but I have a brother who plays music all day."

"What kind?"

"Loud."

The guys smiled. "Well," said Dave, "I don't know much about making music, but I guess we should make some tracks. Let's go."

Jake was still smiling as he walked out of the parking lot. These guys are okay, he thought. When they started their warm-up run through the woods, though, a familiar hard knot started to form in his stomach. What causes that? he wondered. Again, Jake followed just behind Sam. He knew he could pass him when the time came. After the warm-up, Dave met them in the parking lot and had them take off their spikes and put their regular running shoes back on. What now? thought Jake.

"No wind sprints today?" he asked.

"No, that's Wind Sprint Wednesday," answered Shawn. "Today is Far Out Friday."

Far Out Friday? Jake winced. Again, he felt a little like he was in kindergarten. "Did Dave come up with those names?"

"No, we did."

"What's Monday then?"

"Mixed-up Monday. You never know what Dave will come up with. A little bit of anything."

It turned out that Far Out Friday meant they went for a long run across the city. The guys waved at everyone as they jogged by. Jake got the impression they took this route often and had gotten to know certain people as regulars. The lady walking four dogs. The delivery man dropping off boxes at the market. When they passed Ben's Bakery, they all banged on the front window. "What's that all about?" asked Jake.

"Ben's our sponsor," huffed Paul. "He bought us the shirts and stuff."

Jake quickly scanned the front of his jersey and each sleeve. "How come his name isn't on them?"

"I guess he's not into that. Just wants to help out. So we say thanks every time we run by. Show him we're out here working hard."

The guys had stuck together loosely as a group. Sam and Jake, then Shawn, Tony and Paul close behind. Jake had been ready to pass Sam but wasn't sure of the route they were going to take. Now they were on the way back to Cedar Grove, a hundred meters or so from the entrance to the parking lot, and Jake was ready to make his move. He wanted to show Dave what he could do. A cyclist zoomed by on his left. A flash of fur flew in on his right. A little dog, leash and tongue flapping, ran right in front of him. Jake had to jump to avoid trampling him and came down sideways. He rolled onto the grass and made a grab for the leash. A woman came running up.

"Oh, I'm so sorry! Bitsy, you naughty dog!" she cried. "He saw that bike go by and started to chase it," she explained. "He's ridiculous with bikes. He got away from me. I'm so sorry. Are you all right?"

"Fine," said Jake, handing her the leash.

"Are you sure?"

He nodded. The woman went off, scolding Bitsy. By now, Sam had come back and Paul, Tony and Shawn had caught up.

"Oh, no!" said Paul, shaking his head. "Torpedo Dog. I've met up with him before. He sure sabotaged your run." He reached out a hand to pull Jake up. "You okay?"

"Fine." But when Jake stood and put weight on his left ankle, it didn't exactly feel fine.

"Sure?"

"Yeah. Just got the wind knocked out of me for a minute." He walked with the others back to Cedar Grove.

"Here's my team," said Dave as they turned in. "Good to see you, guys." Dave clapped each of them on the shoulder. "Everyone feeling good?" Everyone looked at Jake. He nodded. They all nodded.

"Okay. Do a light run sometime Saturday if you can. Maybe run off that birthday cake and ice cream." He winked at Tony. Tony groaned. "Take Sunday off. Your body needs a rest. See you Monday."

Jake shook his head. Light runs were not his style. Neither were days off. He'd continue with his own schedule. He went to unlock his bike.

"Hey, Jake?" called Dave.

"Yeah?"

"Are you limping?"

"No."

Dave looked at him with one eyebrow raised.

"Maybe a little." He explained about Bitsy.

"Let's have a look."

Jake gasped softly as he took off his shoe, but he tried to cover it up by clearing his throat.

Dave felt the ankle. "Hmm. Not too bad. Stay off it for the weekend though. Should be okay by Monday."

"Okay," said Jake. But he had no intention of taking the weekend off. This would be the perfect test to see if he could tough it out.

Chapter Thirteen

At Monday's practice, Dave had all the boys sit at
the picnic table next to the fence. Jake was glad to
sit down. He stretched his legs out under the table.
He wondered what Dave would ask them to do today.
Mixed-up Monday. Could be anything. He could feel
his ankle throbbing. He'd thought about taping it but
knew that would give him away. He figured if he just
tied his spikes tight enough, he should be okay. Tough
it out, he thought. But it hurt.

Dave stood at one end of the table, put a foot up
on the bench and started by asking each of them how
their weekend had gone. Tony had survived the twins'
birthday party, but just barely. Shawn had had a video
game-and-pizza party. Sam had gone to his brother's

high-school science fair. Paul had nailed his rendition of the *Star Wars* theme at the recital and then spent the rest of the weekend making a log cabin for Social Studies. He showed them the poison ivy on his leg from collecting sticks in the woods and the two burns on his fingers from using a glue gun to stick them together. Dave shook his head. "Guess we'll have to take it easy on you today," he said with a laugh.

Jake let out a long, slow sigh. He hoped that meant the practice would be easy on everyone.

"What about you, Jake?" asked Dave. "Good weekend?"

"Oh." Jake smiled, then shrugged. "Not bad." He didn't want to say he'd been running, and he couldn't think of anything else.

Dave nodded. "Okay, gents, today we're going to talk a little bit about something called bonking."

Shawn pretended to cuff Paul on the side of the head. "Bonk."

Tony slid his shoulder into Sam's on one side, then into Jake's on the other. "Bonk."

Dave laughed. "Not that kind of bonking. What I'm referring to is that feeling of hitting a wall in your race. You can get to a point when you feel you just can't go any further. Your brain tells your legs to quit. Or your legs tell your brain, *That's it, we're done.*" The boys nodded. They knew how that felt.

"Now, some of this is physical," continued Dave. "It has to do with diet, especially with what you ate in the days and the hours before the race. And also if you've had enough to drink and just what it was you filled your tank up with. You guys know all about this, but sometimes you still have to remind yourselves to do it, to choose the right stuff and to get enough of it at the right time."

Jake considered telling them about the pickle juice but decided he'd keep that to himself for now.

"A big part of bonking is also mental. Picture one of Shawn's video games. Sometimes it seems your character is stuck in whatever world he's in, but if you explore the walls a little, you'll come across a little door to escape through. The same thing happens in running. When you feel you've hit a wall, look for that little door. Don't quit. Tell yourself it's there, and you'll probably find it. You boys understand what I'm talking about?"

"Sure, Dave." They nodded.

"Okay then."

They got up from the picnic table and did some stretching. "We're going to start with a light run today," said Dave, clapping Paul lightly on the shoulder. "Follow the paths through twice." Everyone started to jog away. Jake made sure his shoes were tied tightly enough.

"Jake?"

"Yeah?"

"I don't want you to overdo it today. I know you've got the city run tomorrow."

Jake nodded.

"How's that going?"

"Pretty good."

"Ankle okay?"

"Sure. Just a little tender."

Dave's eyebrows went up a little. "Let's see."

Jake loosened the laces again.

"Still a fair bit of swelling," said Dave. "I thought it would be okay after you rested it for the weekend. Hmm. You must have hurt it worse than I thought. Okay. Well, go home then."

"What?" Jake looked up. "It's fine, Dave. I can run. It's fine."

"No, go. You want to be your best for tomorrow, don't you?"

"Yes, but…"

"Then go home, Jake. Put the ankle on ice. Keep it up. Watch a movie or read a book about running if you want to, but don't do any."

"But…"

Dave put a hand on his shoulder. "But nothing. You need to listen to what your body is telling you. Go home and rest. Don't worry. A day off won't hurt your race any."

"It won't?"

"No, but a bum ankle will."

By seven thirty that evening, Jake had had enough of hanging around the house. He needed to go for a run. Just a short one. He changed into some running gear and was tying his shoes when the phone rang.

"Hello?"

"Jake?"

"Yes."

"Dave Driscoll."

"Hi, Dave."

"Just checking that you're staying off that foot."

"Absolutely. Just sitting here watching *Chariots of Fire*."

"Great."

How did he do that?

Jake's mom came through the kitchen. "*Chariots of Fire*? I love that movie. Mind if I watch it with you, Jake?"

Twenty minutes into it, his dad came in too. Then Luke. Halfway through, they paused the disc and made popcorn. They hadn't had a movie night in ages.

"I just love that story," Jake's mom said with a sigh when it was over. She stood up to put the popcorn bowl and glasses on a tray. "And the music." Jake's dad was snoring in one of the La-Z-Boys. Luke was asleep and snoring too, sprawled over one end of the couch. "Not that kind of music," she said as she threw a cushion at each of them. "Rise and shine, fellas!"

"That reminds me," she said. "Jake, I got an email today from Mrs. Bradley. She says she's caught you sleeping in class a couple of times in the last few weeks. She wonders if you're getting enough sleep or if there's something bothering you that's keeping you awake at night."

"I get lots of sleep," protested Jake. "I make sure I get lots of sleep."

"I know you do."

Jake's dad stood up and stretched. "I know he does too. Cut out of the hockey game the other night before the second period was over to make sure he got to bed on time! He shoots, he snores!"

"Maybe it's those early-morning runs. Maybe you're running too much. If it's affecting your schoolwork…"

"Mom, it was probably during math class. Sam's the mathamagician, not me."

"Who's Sam?"

"My fr—" He stopped. "This guy I know from the running club. And maybe it happened once in grammar. I don't mean to. Nouns and pronouns are just not that exciting, you know."

Luke looked up groggily. "It's unavoidable," he agreed. "It's the number slumber."

"The comma coma," said Jake.

Luke nodded. "I've been known to catch a few z's in class myself."

Everyone laughed.

Chapter Fourteen

It was the last of the city league's regular Tuesday runs. Jake looked up and down the starting line, but there were no green spikes. Spencer wasn't there. Jake saw a flash of red and guessed Simon was in the crowd. He didn't go talk to him. He needed to focus. He would find Simon later.

Jake was ready. He'd had a snack. He'd had a drink. He'd done lots of stretching. After resting the ankle last night, he had to admit it felt a lot better. This was it. He felt good. He took a few deep breaths and took his spot at the line. As he did, he felt a weight settle onto his shoulders. Stay loose, he thought. Shake it off. But he couldn't. He took off right at the gun. He got out front early. He ducked the low-hanging branches in the woods. He tuned out the dull ache in his head, the burning in his lungs and the twisting in his stomach. He tuned out the shouts of the fans along the course. He tuned out everything and just ran without thinking, without feeling, one step in front of the other. Through the trees. Along the creek. One foot in front of the other, until he heard the crunch of his spikes on the gravel just before the bridge. Up the hill. Across the finish line. He was all alone. He had won, but without Spencer in the pack, it still felt like second.

Jake didn't wait for the results to be posted. He didn't go look for Simon either. He just didn't feel like waiting today. He pulled a sweatshirt over his head and was unlocking his bike when he heard someone call his name. "Hey, Jake!" He turned. It was Dave. "Great run!"

Jake stood and shook the hand Dave was offering. "Uh, thanks. Recruiting again?"

Dave smiled and clapped Jake on the shoulder. "No. I can do that over the phone. I came to see you."

"Me? Do you need to tell me something about Saturday? I'll be at practice tomorrow."

He shook his head. "No. I came to see you run. The rest of the guys are here too, somewhere."

He looked back at the woods. No one. He looked back at Jake. "You okay?"

"Sure, I guess. Just tired."

"Ankle must feel better."

"Yeah. It's good."

"That's great."

"Yeah."

"Jake?"

"Yeah?"

"You don't look like the guy who just won the race."

Jake shrugged.

"No big grin? No happy dance?"

Jake shrugged again. Dave waited. "There's another guy who's faster than me. Spencer Solomon. He wasn't here today. He probably would have won."

"Spencer, huh." Dave watched him a minute and then asked, "Jake, do you like running?"

"Yeah, I love running."

"Yeah?"

"Or at least I used to, until…"

"Until what?"

"Nothing."

"Until what?"

Jake shrugged.

Dave waited. "Just throw it out there and we'll see where it lands."

"Until…" Jake looked up at Dave and took a deep breath. "Until I started winning."

"Ah." They were both quiet for a moment. "And why is that?"

"I don't know. It wasn't fun anymore after that. I used to just run everywhere because…because— I don't know. Because it was the fastest way to get places, I guess. When I got to my new school a couple years ago, I found out it had a cross-country team. I asked if I could join, and my mom said it sounded like a great thing for me to do. I used to just grab a chocolate bar and make sure my shoes were tied and get out there and run. Then I started to win. Instead of just running, I was thinking about winning all the time. If I would win. What I had to do to win. I do a lot of training, and I watch what I eat and I read all the latest running news. It takes up all my time."

"You do all the right things. But are you doing them for the right reasons?"

Jake shrugged. "Isn't winning a good reason?"

Dave smiled. "Do you feel good running?"

Jake looked up.

Dave tried to explain. "Besides the tough workout it gives you. Do you feel good when you're out there on the course, breathing in, breathing out, watching the world go by?"

"No. I always feel like I have knots in my stomach, and my head hurts."

"And when you're done?"

"I feel...I don't know, heavy."

"Hmm. What did you wear when you ran today?"

Jake looked puzzled. Dave had seen him run. "Just the T-shirt and shorts."

"It's a little nippy out today. No long pants? No winter coat?"

"No."

"Why not?"

Jake didn't answer. All that stuff would be too heavy and wouldn't let him move. Dave knew this.

"What's the solution?" asked Dave after a pause.

"I don't know. I don't think there is one."

"Running isn't fun anymore and you feel lousy before, during and after the race, even when you win."

"Yeah, that about sums it up."

"So stop."

Jake was surprised. "Stop?"

"Yeah. Stop."

"Stop running?"

"No."

"Stop winning?"

Dave laughed. "No."

"What then?"

"Stop running to win."

Jake looked confused. "I don't understand."

"Run to run, Jake. Run the best way you can. Winning will take care of itself."

At that moment Shawn, Sam, Tony and Paul came tumbling out of the woods, all holding snow cones.

"Snow cones?" Dave grinned and shook his head. "You guys are crazy. It's penguin weather out here. What you need is some hot chocolate."

"But snow cones are the best!" answered Tony. "Sorry we took so long. Paul couldn't decide if he wanted blue raspberry or lemon-lime!"

"Great run, Jake," said Sam. They all clapped him on the back.

"Hey, guys. I didn't expect to see you here."

"Here's your snow cone, man. Everybody knows blue raspberry is the way to go," said Shawn, rolling his eyes at Paul's lemon-lime cone.

"You didn't have to do that."

"What do you mean? We wouldn't leave you out. You're one of us! We're a team."

Jake wasn't sure how snow cones fit into his diet. He tried his. It sure tasted good. Cold and sharp. It cut right through the lingering taste of pickles. As he leaned against the bike rack, shivering happily with the other guys and their snow cones, Jake thought he saw a familiar green Jetta turn out of the lot. Then again, a lot of people probably drove green Jettas.

Chapter Fifteen

Jake thought a lot about what Dave had said. *Run to run. Winning will take care of itself.* He had won the last race, hadn't he? Why not enjoy it? He couldn't shake what Simon had said either. *Love what you love.* He did love running. Or he used to. There had to be a way he could get that back.

The team had done a serious practice on Wind Sprint Wednesday. Jake had logged two long runs on Thursday. Now it was Friday, and Dave had told them to take the night off. Jake wasn't used to that yet. It didn't seem right to him. But Dave had said he didn't want to risk anyone getting hurt the day before the regional run, especially since Torpedo Dog could be lurking anywhere. That made sense. Still, Jake felt like running.

He'd go easy. It would be for fun. He wasn't going to worry about anything. Not his time. Not the distance. Not the run tomorrow. Not the championship run on Tuesday. Not Spencer. *Especially* not Spencer.

He changed into some running gear, and on his way downstairs he saw Luke in his room. Jake paused, then knocked on the half-open door. "Hey, Luke. You want to come for a run with me?"

Luke pulled aside his headphones. "Say what, little bro?"

"I was wondering if you want to come for a run with me."

Luke grinned. "Me?"

"Yeah."

"Run?"

"Yeah."

"Are you nuts?"

Jake laughed. "Okay then." He turned to go downstairs but then returned to the half-open door. "Hey, you've got all your stuff back up here now."

"Yep."

"How come I don't hear you playing?"

"Dad bought these heavy-duty headphones. Now I can play without anyone else hearing it."

"Dad got you headphones?"

"I'm using them, yes, but I think he actually got them for you."

"Oh."

Jake made his way to the back door and put on his shoes. His mother was in the kitchen making tea. "Mom?" He cleared his throat. "Do you know if Dad's been coming out to the Tuesday runs?"

"Tuesday runs?" She tried to pretend she didn't know what he was talking about.

"Mom?"

She put down the teapot and leaned against the counter. "Yes, Jake. He's been going to the Tuesday runs."

"How come he never said anything?"

"He didn't want to—what was the word?—distract you."

"Oh."

The door to Jake's dad's workshop behind the garage was half open too. His dad was whistling as he sanded something.

"Dad?"

"Jake-O."

"Luke showed me his headphones."

"Uh-huh."

"They seem to work well."

"Yep."

"Dad?"

"Yes?"

"Nothing, I guess."

"You going for a run again, Jake? Be careful."

Jake nodded. "Do you, ah, want to come with me?"

His dad looked up. He looked alarmed.

Jake laughed. "Never mind."

It was definitely frosty outside, but for some reason Jake felt warm inside. He zipped up his jacket, tugged on his winter hat and started out at a leisurely pace, trying to take in all the scenery. Most of the trees had lost all their leaves. There were still piles of them here and there, and they gave off a heavy smell. Jake heard laughter and shouting. Kids were playing road hockey. The streetlights glowed and soft yellow light warmed the windows all along the street.

After fifteen minutes, Jake decided he'd gone far enough. He jogged back home, passing the new restaurant on the corner. Sl'ice. A big banner was plastered across the front. *Now Open*. Jake stopped and looked in. Bright chrome countertops. Pizza offered on one side.

Ice cream on the other. Cheery red-checkered table-cloths. Maybe he'd tell his family they should come and try it. It was busy. Jake noticed a family just finishing their dinner. It looked like they were having a nice time together. Mom, Dad, sister, brother. They all laughed at something the father said, then stood to pull on their jackets. Yes, thought Jake. He would ask his parents if they could come for dinner one night. It should be okay to bend the food rules one time. It would be fun to have a night out with his family. Jake smiled and stepped out of the way as the family left the restaurant. When the young boy passed him, though, Jake's warm feeling drained away. It was Spencer.

So, Spencer Solomon was back in action. Would he be at the championship run on Tuesday? Jake was sure he would be. He would have to be ready. Jake had planned to go in, but instead he ran right past his house. He picked up the pace and clocked another few kilometers. This was no time for fooling around.

Chapter Sixteen

Saturday was cold but clear. When the team had assembled at Cedar Grove, Dave handed out new warm-up suits from their sponsor. Slick. They were black, with the Diamond logo in blue and silver on the back of the jacket. They were perfect for a day like this one. The race was at 1:00 PM. It was an hour's ride away. They left at ten. Dave drove them up in his van. They talked about the weather, school, movies. Shawn, sitting up front with Dave, seemed to be explaining the highlights of every video game ever made. Paul and Tony started a game of Would You Rather.

"Would you rather be a penguin or a giraffe?"

"Would you rather live at the North Pole or at the equator?"

"Would you rather get caught in a sandstorm or fall in quicksand?"

"Would you rather eat a cheeseburger with chocolate sauce on it or a pancake soaked in pickle juice?"

"Oh, man, does anyone else smell pickles?" asked Tony. "I'm hungry."

Paul laughed. "You're always hungry." He asked the next question. "Would you rather do a thousand math questions or be thrown in a den of lions?"

"Lions," answered Tony with a grin, punching Sam lightly on the arm.

"Would you rather get attacked by a shark or gored by a warthog?"

What kind of a question was that? Jake would rather they stopped playing for a while. He was trying to focus, to prepare for the race, to get in the zone, but they just kept talking. And talking. And talking. All except Sam. He was working on a Sudoku.

"Ah, Dave?" piped up Jake when there was a lull in the gaming conversation.

"Yessir?"

"Isn't there anything we should be doing now to prepare for the race?"

"No. Just relax, I guess."

"Well, do we know who the main competition is?"

Dave's eyes flicked to the rearview mirror to scan the back of the van. "It's a big race," he commented, "but I don't want you guys to worry about that. I just want you to do your best. There will be a lot of runners, but they aren't the enemy. They're just other guys out there doing their best."

The park in Deep Rapids was a busy place. Convenors and course monitors were giving and getting instructions. Coaches were reading clipboards or chatting. Groups of runners were walking and stretching. Parents were warming up with coffee and hot chocolate. The yellow caution tape marking parts of the course flapped in the stiff breeze, and the bright-orange pylons indicating turns flashed in the sun.

The boys went with Dave to register and pick up their numbers. Dave had brought along a small tent to keep their gear in, and they pitched it under a huge tree. Dave led them through a long set of stretches, and they had a light snack. Then they did a walk-through of the course together.

"Pay attention, amigos," said Dave. "We don't want anyone to get lost."

"Just follow the guy in front of you," joked Shawn.

"What if he's lost?" Dave laughed.

Jake took everything in. Every detail. He had every intention of being the one out front.

The starting line stretched across a large field next to a picnic shelter. They would run the length of the field and then follow a path around a huge pond where there were hundreds of ducks. It was going to be important to cross that field quickly so they wouldn't get caught in the bottleneck at the trailhead. After the pond, the trail wound through the woods. It was narrow there. It would be hard to pass anyone on that stretch. Then it opened out along the lakeshore, where there was lots of space, but it was going to be tough running in the sand, and the wind was brutal out in the open. After a section of small hills back in the trees, runners would return to the field from the other end and run through a tape-marked trough up to the finish at the picnic shelter. "Remember," said Dave. "You're not finished when you reach the tape. Don't stop pumping until you cross the line."

Dave had them warm up with a few short runs and some strides across the field. "Get a drink, guys," he called, "and then come on in for a huddle." It was twelve forty-five.

The Diamond team stood together in a circle, arms across each other's shoulders. Dave grinned. "Well, here we are. You boys have worked hard, and you are ready for this. You're ready here." He pointed to his feet. "And here." He tapped his temple. "And here." He put one hand over his heart. "You can do this. Run hard. Run smart. It's a team event. You're a great team. Do your best! I'm proud of you."

Jake wondered how Dave could be proud of them when they hadn't even run yet. He intended to earn that pride. Just wait until he showed Dave what he could do.

Paul led a loud cheer. "Let's kick up some Diamond Dust!"

Dave shook his head and laughed.

They peeled off their warm-up suits, dropped them in the tent and made their way to the starting line. It sure was chilly. There was a solid wall of runners, two hundred at least, in all different colors of jerseys. Red. Blue. Orange. Yellow. Green. Purple. White. Black. And silver. Dave had the boys line up one behind the other from the line. Sam. Jake. Paul. Shawn. Tony. Paul was jumping up and down. Shawn was doing some sort of deep breathing. Tony cracked his knuckles and looked for a place to throw out his gum. Dave wrapped it up in a receipt he found in his jacket pocket. Sam just stood, silent, waiting. Jake felt tense, but he tried to focus. Mental toughness, he said to himself. Be the toughest one out there.

A big man in a red jacket strode out into the field. "Welcome to the regional race," he boomed through his megaphone. "It is 1:00 PM on my watch, and this is the event for twelve-year-old boys. You've all been through the course—and if you haven't, you'll get your chance shortly!" He chuckled. "I wish you well. Runners, please take your marks."

Jake took a deep breath and moved in behind Sam. "Get set."

Focus. Focus. A good start was key.

Bang. The gun went off and the line surged ahead.

Sam sprinted across the field, and Jake made sure to stay right behind him. They moved with about twenty runners to the head of the pack and found a place on the path around the pond. Jake heard someone huffing and puffing beside him and looked over to find Paul grinning wildly as he passed him. Jake was tempted to sprint up to him, but it didn't feel right. It was too fast. If he ran that way now, he'd have nothing left later.

Jake struggled to find a good rhythm. He tucked back in behind Sam and tried to steady himself. Flocks of ducks exploded into the air as the runners pounded around the first turn. There were six, maybe seven, runners ahead of Sam. The pond, the trees, the lake, the hills, chanted Jake to himself. The pond, the trees, the lake, the hills.

They had almost completed the loop around the water and were looking to head into the woods when Jake saw Sam veer right to pass. Jake followed. It was Paul. He wasn't grinning anymore and was running with one hand clenched hard to his side, like he had a cramp.

I knew it was too fast, thought Jake.

"Stay in it, Paul," called Sam. "Go Diamond."

That left six guys to pass.

The trees, the lake, the hills, the field, thought Jake, panting. The trees, the lake, the hills, the field.

"Looking great, guys!" a voice called out. Jake jumped. There was Dave, stepping out from among the trees alongside the trail. How did he get there? "There's a bit of a clearing up ahead, if you can use it."

Breathe in, breathe out. In, out, in, out. Arms pumping, legs beginning to burn. *Focus. Focus.*

The trail did widen out a bit, as Dave had said, and Sam used the opportunity to pass the runner in front of him and slide back into position just before it narrowed again. Smooth, thought Jake. He had moved right with him. Five left out front. *Watch out for rocks, for roots, for low-hanging branches. In, out, in, out.* All the way through the woods.

They felt the temperature change as they charged out onto the beach. Angry waves pounded the shore, and the wind slapped at them and tore at the numbers pinned to their jerseys. The coarse sand churned under their feet. *The lake, the hills, the field, the trough. The lake, the hills, the field, the trough.* Jake's calf muscles screamed at him to pack it in. His shoulders hurt. His lungs ached. Bonk. Bonk. Where's that little door? he asked himself. Find that little door. He was breathing hard. Squinting against the wind and the sand made his head hurt. Then Dave stepped out from behind a huge rock. "That's it, fellas! How's this for wind sprints? Keep it up. More of the same. You've got this." His hood was tied so tightly that his face was all scrunched up. Jake laughed out loud. Man, that looked funny. But Dave's voice was loud and clear, and Jake suddenly felt stronger.

Jake moved slightly to the right to get out of the spray of sand Sam was kicking up. Just ahead were the pylons marking the entrance to the trail through the trees. He'd be out of the wind and back on firm ground. Jake felt a charge of energy. Just a little bit farther to the trees. He followed as Sam kicked in with a quick burst of speed to pass two runners just ahead of the pylons. Three left in the lead.

The change to being out of the wind was so sudden, Jake almost fell over. After all that fighting, he felt like he was floating. *Switch gears. Short strides up the hills, longer steps down. The hills, the field, the trough, the finish. The hills, the field, the trough, the finish. Keep going. Keep going. One foot in front of the other. Breathe in. Breathe out.* Jake stayed focused on the silver jersey in front of him. *Steady. Steady.* Then Sam caught a root and stumbled. He threw his hands out in front of him and was up again in an instant. Behind him, Jake jumped the root and pulled even.

"Keep going, Jake," said Sam.

Jake looked over at him. Sam waved him on as he tried to find his rhythm again. There was a flicker of pain in his eyes. Should I stop? thought Jake. I should wait, make sure Sam is all right.

"I'm okay," Sam panted. "Keep going, Jake. Go for it." Sam nodded. Jake hesitated for a split second, then nodded back. "Go Diamond," called Sam as Jake took off.

He sprinted up behind a small kid in a yellow jersey. For a short time they were matched stride for stride, but Jake's stride was longer and he soon moved in front. A white shirt and a red one were all that remained. *Up, down, up, down. In, out, in, out. Focus. Focus.* Jake pulled up behind the runner in white. He had a good rhythm going, but his breathing was pretty ragged. Looking to his right, Jake saw sunlight streaming through the trees and realized they were coming up along the field already. *The field, the turn, the trough, the finish. Dig. Dig deep.* He launched himself off his toes and pulled past the white shirt. One more.

This guy was a great runner. No wonder he was out front. His movements were smooth and fluid. His stride was even and his breathing controlled. Over a black long-sleeved shirt, he wore a red jersey with some type of logo on the back that Jake couldn't make out, and he had a black knit hat on his head. Step it up, Jake told himself. Step it up just a little.

They were in the field now, coming up on the turn into the tape. Dave leaned in from where he stood along the side. "Let it all out now, Jake. It's time. Let it go!"

Jake's legs felt like logs. His lungs were on fire. Bulldogs, he thought. That's what it said on the back of that guy's jersey: *Bulldogs*. He could read it now! He was that close. *The turn, the trough, the finish. The turn, the trough, the finish. Dig, dig, dig, dig.* Jake found another gear and started to sprint. They were in the trough now, tape flapping on either side. He pulled up next to the red runner. Their arms were pumping, their legs were churning. *Run. Run. Run to run. Run to run.* Jake felt like a weight was slowly lifting off him. He looked up at the blue sky and sucked in the cold air and found himself grinning. He didn't think about the other guy. He didn't think about his legs. He didn't think about his lungs. He didn't feel the ache in his shoulders. He didn't feel anything but free. And fast. *Run. Run. Don't stop running until you cross the line. Don't stop running. Don't stop. Don't.* Jake summoned every little bit of energy he could find left inside and flew across the finish line. First. First place. Jake Jarvis.

Chapter Seventeen

Jake walked around a bit behind the finish line to get his wind back. He wasn't tired at all. He felt light, excited. He made his way over to the big tree they had made home base. He did some stretches and a quick little happy dance and reached into the tent for his jacket and some water. He heard his name and saw someone jogging toward him. Simon.

"Jake, that was awesome!"

"Simon, what are you doing here?"

"Watching the race."

"Yeah, but…" Jake reddened a little. He hadn't told Simon about the race today. He hadn't even told him about running with the Diamond Club.

"I read about it in the paper. I saw your name. I wanted to go, and my mom said she wouldn't mind shopping in Deep Rapids for an afternoon. She'll pick me up later."

"You wanted to come all the way out here for a race you're not even in?"

Simon stared at Jake for an instant and smiled. "We're friends, aren't we?"

Then Dave and Sam came up, with Shawn between them. Paul was behind them. Shawn's left leg, elbow, shoulder, chin and cheekbone were all scraped up. "Shawn! Are you all right?"

"Looks worse than it feels, I think, although it doesn't feel so great either."

"What happened?"

"Colossal wipeout."

"Was it a root?" asked Sam.

"No."

"Rock?" asked Paul.

"No."

"Foot?" asked Jake.

"No."

"Branch?" asked Simon.

"Negative, dudes. It happened way back by the pond. I slipped on some gooey duck guck and took a major dive."

"Gross!"

"Awesome!"

"Whoa."

"But he didn't quit," said Dave. "Took all that scuffing and still came in at fifty-four. Well done, Shawn."

The whole team crowded in to pat Shawn on the back.

"Ouch," he bellowed. "Ouch, ouch, ouch!"

"Sorry, man."

Shawn looked at Paul and Sam and Jake. "How'd you guys do?

"Or doo-doo, maybe?" offered Simon. Jake winced. Not the jokes! He hadn't even had a chance to introduce Simon to the guys yet. The rest of the boys laughed.

"Twenty-nine," said Paul.

"Solid."

"Fifth," said Sam.

Shawn's eyebrows shot up. "Nice." He turned to Jake. "You?"

Jake wasn't sure what to do. The superhero pose didn't feel right this time. Before he could say anything, someone else did.

"Numero uno," piped up Simon. "My friend Jake here was the first across the line."

Everyone stood silently for a moment. Then they all cheered wildly.

"No way!" shouted Paul.

"Awesome," said Sam, nodding.

"My man!" echoed Shawn.

"Leavin' 'em in the Diamond dust," said Paul.

Dave laughed. "It was quite some finish, Jake. What was that all about?"

"I was just running."

"Yeah?"

"I had somewhere to go."

"And it seemed the fastest way to get there?"

"I guess so."

"Well, buddy, I'd say you definitely got there!" They all grinned ridiculously. There were high fives all around. Even for Simon.

"Sit for a bit, Shawn," advised Dave. "Then we'll get you cleaned up. We're just waiting for Tony to come in."

Dave jogged off toward the finish line. Paul ran over to the score sheets plastered to the fence. Sam explained how it worked. Because it was a team event, all the runners' results counted toward the total. The team with the lowest total score would win. Paul jogged back waving a napkin excitedly in his hand.

"Guys," he panted. "I think we have a shot at top three. Look, I wrote the numbers down. The guys from Fletcher—they're the ones in yellow—are all in: 4, 22, 23, 67, and 71."

Sam added the numbers in his head. "That's 187 points."

"Whoa. How do you do that?" asked Shawn. "What do we have?"

"Eighty-nine, so far."

"But wait," said Paul. "Red—that's the Bulldogs—they look good too. They have runners at 2, 10, 17, and 62."

"Ninety-one," whispered Sam. "And we both have one more runner coming in."

"What does it mean?" asked the others.

"It means it's going to be close!"

"Tony!" They all rushed over to the tape.

"Wait for me," hollered Shawn, hobbling along behind them. "I don't want to miss this!"

Runners were finishing in groups of two and three, racing each other through the trough. The display board read *75* as a runner in a black jersey crossed the line. White. Purple. Where was Tony? There! A group of five had turned into the trough. Two green shirts, a red shirt, a silver and a blue.

"C'mon, Tony!" they all yelled. "C'mon!"

Five runners hurtled through the trough, legs flying, arms pumping. Red was ahead. Then green. Now blue.

"C'mon, Tony!"

Face flushed, he pushed across the line. The board flashed *81*. Would it be enough?

The Diamond team surrounded Tony at the finish and clapped him on the back.

"Paul," called Sam. "Go find out how the Bulldog runner finished."

They waited anxiously as Paul scurried off toward the sheets. Runners were still finishing, but yellow was all in: 4, 22, 23, 67, 71. Silver, all in: 1, 5, 29, 54, 81. Red. What about red? 2, 10, 17, 62 and what?

"We've got 1 and 5," said Shawn. "That's got to be enough to take their 2 and 10, don't you think?"

"I don't know. I don't know," replied Sam.

"Seventy-eight," yelled Paul, coming across the field. "He came in at 78."

Everyone looked at Sam.

"2, 10, 17, 62, 78…Guys—we did it. We did it!"

A loud cheer went up from the circle of boys in silver shirts. Sam grinned. Paul jumped. Shawn whooped. Tony grabbed Jake's wrist and pulled Jake's arm up with his.

"I can't believe it!" shouted Sam. "Top three! Yellow has 187 points. We have 170. Red has 169. We've got second place!"

Jake froze. Second? Second? He hated second. He thought he was done being second. No way. He had finished first. First.

Jake pulled his arm down. Just then Dave jogged over. "Unbelievable! Do you guys know…?"

"We know! Second place!" hollered Paul. "Sam figured it out for us."

Dave laughed. He winked at Sam. "Unbelievable," he said again. "Well done, boys! Well done! I need to talk to you about a few things, and I think there's some hardware coming your way, but first I want you to do a bit of a cool-down. Shawn, you come with me to the first-aid tent. The rest of you guys, take an easy jog away from the course. Meet you by our tent in, say, twenty minutes."

Jake jogged away toward the lake. He figured no one else would head that way, and he wanted to be by himself. He faced into the wind and tried to clear his head. His chest felt tight, and he had a hard lump in his throat. The team had missed first place by one point. One. If any one of the guys had run just a little bit faster and passed one more runner, they could have tied for first or had it all on their own. He was the only one who couldn't have done that. There was no one left for him to pass. Yet everyone seemed so happy. Didn't the rest of these guys want to win? Jake remembered Dave's pre-race pep talk about doing their best. Their best did not seem to be good enough. Maybe they didn't want it enough. What happened to *winning will take care of itself*? Sure, Dave.

As he stood in the cold wind, Jake thought about all the times Dave had popped up along the course, offering advice, encouraging him to give it his all. He knew Dave had done that for all five of them. He thought about Sam running hard to the finish. He thought about Paul starting out way too fast but then pulling it back and running smart. He thought about Shawn crashing but not quitting. He thought about Tony powering his way through the pressure at the end. He thought about the way he had felt running today. And he knew something then. They *had* given it their all. They had run a good race. It wasn't first, but it was their best. And maybe that was okay.

Simon came up behind him. "Jake?"

"Yeah?"

"You okay?"

"Yeah."

"The rest of the guys are waiting for you."

"Okay, I'm coming." He paused. It occurred to him that Simon had given his all too. In more ways than one. Jake turned. "Simon?"

"Yeah?"

"Thanks for making the trip out here."

"It's cool, and I'm not talking temperature. I like running."

Jake smiled. "Me too."

The boys walked up just as the convenor began calling out the names of the top three teams. Dave met them at the tent. "Hustle now, Jake. Go join your team."

Jake moved in quietly beside Sam. For a moment he held on to the silver medal the big man in the red jacket handed him. Then he took a deep breath and slipped it over his head. It felt good.

They took down the tent, picked up their water bottles, said goodbye to Simon, who had to go meet up with his mom, and piled into Dave's van. "Hey, guys, look at this," called Shawn. He lifted a box from the front seat. *BEN'S BAKERY*, it said in big letters on top. Inside were a dozen donuts.

"Awesome!"

"Ben is the best!"

Jake hadn't eaten a donut in ages. They were not part of his regular, carefully regimented, results-oriented diet. He took a chocolate glazed. It was delicious.

"Hey, Jake," said Shawn. "Your friend Simon is a riot. You know what he said when I came back from the first-aid tent looking like a mummy? He said, *Well, it looks like you've got things all wrapped up*. Ha ha!"

"Yeah," agreed Paul. "He's got a joke for all occasions. Bring him again."

Jake smiled. They all settled sleepily into their seats.

"Dave," asked Sam as they pulled out onto the highway, his mouth half full of donut, "wasn't there something you wanted to talk about?"

"Oh, right." Dave smiled. He glanced in the rearview mirror. "Just a small item of information I wanted to pass on. The winners here today? They get to go on to the provincials."

"Oh," mumbled Tony. "Good for those Bulldogs."

"The race is next Saturday."

"Guess they'll be working hard this week," said Paul.

"It's up north this year, about five hours from here," continued Dave. "It'll be a whole weekend away."

It got very quiet in the van. Jake closed his eyes. He would have loved to be going to that provincial race. Oh well. He tried to erase the disappointment from his face, but when he opened his eyes again, he saw the same look on the faces of all four of his friends.

Finally Sam piped up, "Sounds like fun."

"Yeah," said Shawn. "Up north, huh? Better bring their woollies."

Dave cleared his throat. "The top two teams qualify."

They all sat bolt upright in their seats. "What?"

♦ ♦ ♦

Dave dropped all the boys off at home. He told them he'd get them the information about the provincial race as soon as he had it. When he got inside, Jake found his parents having coffee at the kitchen table.

"How'd it go, Jake?"

"Well…" He grinned and showed them the silver medal. They grinned back.

"Fabulous!" said his mother.

"How'd it feel?" asked his dad.

"Good." Jake sat down with them. "It was a good run." He looked up from the medal. "There's another race this coming week, the championship run for the city league. It's Tuesday, if you want to come."

"I'd like that," said his dad. "I'll be there." He looked over at Jake's mom, and she nodded. "Listen, Jake, you've been working so hard and doing so well. We'd like to give you something. We were thinking you could use a new pair of shoes."

"Really?" Jake thought for a moment. "You know what? I kind of like mine. I've finally got them worn in just right. But I have another idea. How about pizza at Sl-ice, all four of us? Tonight?"

"You're on."

Jake smiled. He figured he'd wait until then to share his news about the provincials.

Jake took a shower and then slept for an hour. Just before they left for the restaurant, he got a call from Dave. "Listen, Jake. I don't want you to come to Monday's practice."

"What? Why not?"

"You've got your championship race on Tuesday. Focus on that."

"Oh. Okay. But what about the provincials?"

"Let's not talk about that yet. I should know all I need to know by Tuesday. Do some light runs maybe. Lots of stretching. Stay out of the line of fire of any crazy dogs, okay? Or ducks, I guess. And Jake? Good job today."

"Thanks."

Jake hung up the phone slowly. Exactly what was it Dave would know by Tuesday? Maybe he only needed a team of four, and since Jake was the fifth runner to join the team…Something felt a little funny. Jake decided to hold off telling his family about the run on Saturday until he had spoken with Dave again.

Chapter Eighteen

Jake ran through the rain Monday morning, tried hard not to sleep through adverbs and adjectives and did some weights that night. It felt weird not being out with the team. He did a light run on Tuesday morning. After school he put on a T-shirt and shorts and pulled some sweats on over top. He missed wearing the Diamond jersey and the warm-up suit, but he knew he was just running for himself today. Better yet, he was just running today. Just running to run. At least, he'd try.

It was cold. Jake made sure he did lots of stretching and didn't take off his hat or sweats until they had called everyone to the starting line. This was it. Simon was there. Spencer was there too. Jake saw his dad in the crowd and got a thumbs-up. He saw Dave and caught another one. Okay. *Run to run*. He took a deep breath and took his place at the line. No knots in his stomach. No weight on his shoulders. Jake smiled.

He jumped right with the gun and got off to a great start. Spencer, Max and a few others pulled ahead early. Not too fast, thought Jake. Not too fast. Just stick with the others. Watch out for obstacles. He ran steadily, pulling in the cold air. Through the woods. Along the creek. Jake saw ice had formed along the edges. A flock of geese flew noisily overhead. His ears were burning and his fingers tingled, but Jake felt good. He felt strong. He passed a guy in black. He passed Max.

He could just see the pylons ahead of the bridge when he pulled even with Spencer. They were running in sync, matched stride for stride. They looked at each other as they crossed the bridge, grinned, nodded and took off in a sprint up the hill toward the finish. Jake felt the same surge of energy he'd had running through the tape in Deep Rapids. *Dig. Dig. Dig. Dig. Go. Go. Go. Go.* Side by side they ran. People were yelling. *One, two, one, two, up to the finish*. Finished. Spencer was first, but there wasn't even a second between them. It was that close.

Jake felt empty and full at the same time. His first thought was that Spencer Solomon was a very good runner. His second thought was that he'd really like some water. His dad came up, slugged his shoulder and handed him a water bottle. "Well done, Jakey. Well done."

"Thanks, Dad."

The guys from the Diamond team swarmed him seconds later, patting him on the back and giving him high fives. Tony, Shawn, Sam. Paul must have had trombone practice or something.

"That was some cool running, Jake. Hey, guys, we've got to celebrate," said Tony. "You think they still have snow cones?"

They laughed and shivered. "I could go for some hot chocolate," said Jake, "but I want to see Simon come in. He's trying to break the top twenty today."

They all waited and watched and cheered as Simon came in. Tony, Sam and Shawn tackled him on the other side of the finish line. "Dude, your face is as red as your shirt!" said Shawn, laughing.

Jake went over to shake his hand. "Good run, Simon."

"Thanks, Jake. You too?"

"Yeah, me two." He held up two fingers.

"Sweet! Whew," Simon panted, "I'm whipped. Fried. Pooped!" He stopped and shook his head. He put his hands together and bowed to Shawn. "Apologies," he said. "I think the only one who may say that is a true veteran of the duck pond."

They roared.

"I'm going to see where I end up on that board," huffed Simon. "I've got high hopes for today." The boys moved toward the parking lot. "Coming, Jake?"

"Ah, I'll catch up to you in just a minute," answered Jake. He felt he still owed one more handshake. Where was Spencer? He scanned the crowd. There. Suddenly Jake felt like a blast of cold air had hit him, and it wasn't just the November weather. Dave Driscoll had beaten him to it and was shaking Spencer Solomon's hand. Now Jake understood why Dave had told him not to come to practice Monday and why he hadn't wanted to talk about the provincial competition. He was waiting for the results of this race. He was going to go with Spencer.

It made sense. Spencer was a great runner. The best. But still...Dave laughed at something Spencer said and then turned. He saw Jake and walked over, a big grin on his face. Jake steeled himself for what was coming. He stuck out his hand awkwardly to shake Dave's. "Dave," he blurted, "thank you for asking me to be part of the Diamond team."

Dave looked confused. "I'm glad I did, Jake."

"I understand why you don't need me anymore."

"I don't need you anymore?"

"I completely understand why you're asking me to step aside."

"I'm asking you to step aside? Why am I doing that?"

"It's for the good of the team. With that big race coming up, Spencer's your man."

Dave looked back to where he'd just been chatting with Spencer, and suddenly he understood. He shook his head. He stopped shaking Jake's hand and cuffed him on the shoulder. "Jake, what are you talking about? You're still a member of our team. I'm not ditching you."

"You're not?"

"No way. I was just congratulating Spencer on a great run. Just like I want to congratulate you. Well done!"

Jake let out his breath. He hadn't realized he'd been holding it the whole time. "Thanks, Dave."

"Now, funny thing is, since we're talking about the Diamond team, it does appear that we will need another runner for the provincial race. Seems Paul has come down with the chicken pox. I hear it's been going around. I thought it was just for little kids."

Jake laughed. "Me too. Poor Paul," he said. "He'll have a tough time lying low for a bit." They both nodded. "But Dave, if you have to do some recruiting, I think you should call Spencer."

"Yeah?"

"Yeah. Definitely."

"Okay then. I'll ask him. But I wonder if we can find some sort of job for your friend Simon too. He just seems to be able to keep everybody on the up and up. What do you think?"

"Sounds great."

When Jake and his dad got home, they found the kitchen table covered with boxes.

"How'd it go?" asked his mom.

"Great," answered Jake. "Second."

"Nice finish." She messed up his hair. "Are you all done now?"

Jake looked at his dad and laughed. Behind his back, his dad was holding the piece of paper he'd gotten from Dave, outlining the plans for going to the provincial race on the weekend.

"Almost," he replied. "What's all this?"

"Well," said his mom, "there's a big concert in a couple of weeks, and we're helping to get the word out." The boxes nearest Jake were full of flyers.

"What concert? Is Luke going?" Jake lifted out one of the posters.

"You could say that," she said with a laugh.

Jake looked at the page in his hand. *Youth Concert. Featuring The Cave Dwellers, Pond Scum and Celebrated Solo Guitarist Luke Jarvis.*

Jake's eyes almost popped out of his head. "People want to come and hear Luke play?"

His dad grinned. "He's really not so bad."

"So," explained Jake's mom, "we'll have to get these posters out around town and help with some of the setting up at the hall, but what I really need to do is order some refreshments. I'm not sure who to call. Anyone have a good idea?"

Jake had the perfect suggestion. "Mom," he said, "you should call Ben's Bakery."

"Are they good?"

"The best," insisted Jake.

"Okay then."

"Hey, can I call Simon and invite him to this thing?"

"Absolutely. You might want to make it a sleepover. It's going to be late."

"Tell him we'll make pizza," threw in Jake's dad. "We'll have a movie too."

"That sounds like a great idea!" said Simon when Jake called. But when Simon suggested pickles as one of the toppings to try on their pizza, Jake found he couldn't say the same.

"I've got a good idea for a movie though," offered Jake.

"Spiderman!" they shouted together.

Acknowledgments

Even though my name appears on the cover of *Seconds*, I cannot take all the credit for it coming to be. There are several people I would like to thank. There would have been no book at all without the enthusiasm of Sarah Harvey and the wisdom and encouragement of Amy Collins at Orca Books. There would certainly have been much less excitement without the support of my family. And there would simply have been no story without all of the cross-country runners and coaches I've had the pleasure of cheering for and with over the years. Their determination and dedication proved to be my inspiration. Thank you all.

Way back when she was in grade school, Sylvia Taekema was asked to write about what she would like to do when she grew up. She wrote that she didn't know exactly, but that it would probably have something to do with children. She was right. In addition to all the fun she and her husband have with their own children, Sylvia enjoys working as a supply teacher and as a volunteer in programs for children at school, at church and in the community. She loves to read, bake cookies and go on camping adventures with her family. She lives in Chatham, Ontario.